THE SECRET KEEPERS: JACK'S JOURNAL #1

ALSO BY NELLIE H. STEELE

Cate Kensie Mysteries:
The Secret of Dunhaven Castle
Murder at Dunhaven Castle
Holiday Heist at Dunhaven Castle

Jack's Journal:
Murder in the Tower

Shadow Slayers Stories:
Shadows of the Past
Stolen Portrait Stolen Soul
Gone

Maggie Edwards Adventures
Cleopatra's Tomb
Secret of the Ankhs

Duchess of Blackmoore Mysteries
Death of a Duchess

THE SECRET KEEPERS: JACK'S JOURNAL #1

A CATE KENSIE MYSTERY

NELLIE H. STEELE

A Novel Idea Publishing

This is a work of fiction. Names, characters, places, and incidents either are the product of the author's imagination or are used fictitiously. Any resemblance to actual persons, living or dead, events, or locales is entirely coincidental.

Copyright © 2021 by Nellie H. Steele

All rights reserved.

No part of this book may be reproduced in any form or by any electronic or mechanical means, including information storage and retrieval systems, without written permission from the author, except for the use of brief quotations in a book review.

All rights reserved.

Cover design by Stephanie A. Sovak.

❦ Created with Vellum

ACKNOWLEDGMENTS

A very special thank you to everyone who made this book possible! Special shout outs to: Stephanie Sovak, Paul Sovak, Michelle Cheplic, Mark D'Angelo, Lori D'Angelo and Peter Nicholls.

Finally, a HUGE thank you to you, the reader!

Reid Family Tree

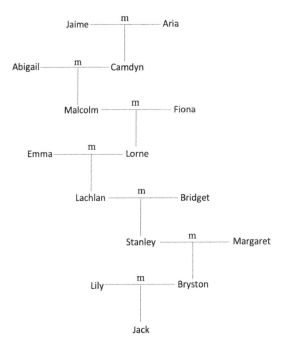

CHAPTER 1

August 18
8:07 a.m.

*H*ello...
 I'm not quite sure where to begin (I've never done this before, kept a journal, that is) but I suppose an introduction is in order. My name is Jack Reid. I live in the town of Dunhaven, Scotland. I'm the estate manager at Dunhaven Castle.

I've started this journal because I've discovered something incredible. Not just me alone. I've got a partner in crime, but I'll explain all that. I'm still reeling from the discovery, actually. I know I shouldn't be writing this all down, but this is the only way I can make any sense of it.

You see, I've just learned that time travel exists. Yeah, time travel. I couldn't believe it either. I still can't most of the time. I've done it. I've time traveled. And I still can't believe it.

I should back up and tell the story from the beginning. I'll start with a little more information about me.

As I mentioned, I'm the estate manager for Dunhaven Castle and one of the caretakers. I only started my position there a few months ago when Lady Gertrude MacKenzie was the proprietor. My father was the estate manager before me and my grandfather before him and so on down the line all the way back to the building of the castle. There's always been a Reid on the estate. I considered it some old-fashioned tradition and nothing more, but that wasn't the case. In addition to groundskeeping, I also schedule all maintenance and inspect the castle to keep everything in tiptop shape.

Six months ago, my father passed away unexpectedly. I wasn't even here. I regret that, but I can't change it. I was off traveling the world, making my own mark. Or so I thought.

I returned home after that. Too late for my father, but not for my grandfather. I took my father's position on the estate. "Doing my duty as a Reid," my grandfather told me. Little did I know how much that duty entailed!

About three months into my work at Dunhaven, Lady MacKenzie passed away. Old Gertrude didn't have any known relatives. Lady MacKenzie, that is. She's probably spinning in her grave after I called her "Old Gertrude."

Anyway, she found out she had terminal cancer and passed away shortly after. There wasn't much time to discuss who the castle would be passed to. The other two staff members, Charlie and Emily Fraser, and I wondered what might become of the place. But Mr. Smythe, the estate's attorney, assured us Lady MacKenzie's will contained a provision to find the next proprietor.

The process took months. Lady MacKenzie, an only child, never married and had no children. They had to search through the entire family tree to find her next of kin. And when I say entire family tree, I mean it. They had to go to a distant cousin of a cousin of a cousin. Well, you get the idea.

After months, Mr. Smythe informed us he had found Lady MacKenzie's next of kin, an American! Whew, you should have heard Mrs. Fraser's reaction to that one! The arrival of Lady Catherine Kensie as the castle's new proprietor and the county's newest Countess is really where this story begins.

It was a warm June day when Lady Cate, as we now call her, arrived. Mr. and Mrs. Fraser and I spent the week preparing for her arrival. Mrs. Fraser fretted over what she may do. Would she like us? Hate us? Would she fire us all? Lady Gertrude, stuffy as she may be, always treated the staff kindly. In fact, before her untimely death, she had promised to bequeath the cottage the Frasers live in to them as an early retirement gift. She passed away before the papers could be drawn up. Mrs. Fraser worried she'd not only lose her job with the new owner but perhaps even her home!

Mr. Smythe informed us they would arrive in the late afternoon. My nervous energy kept me busy. Under the cloudless sky, I puttered around the estate, snipping wayward limbs on bushes and smoothing the gravel on the drive. The morning hours dragged by. I checked my watch so many times I began to believe the thing stopped.

The lunch hour arrived, and we gathered in the kitchen for the quietest meal I'd ever experienced on the estate. I estimate we talked more the day of Lady MacKenzie's death than we did on this day. Mrs. Fraser made a large meal. She'd spent the entire morning cooking and baking. Being one of her favorite pastimes, it provided an outlet for her nervousness.

I snacked on another of Mrs. Fraser's biscuits as I pondered the upcoming upheaval. It appeared everyone around the table engaged in the same ponderings. We'd chitchatted about the nice weather, but Lady Cate's impending arrival stilted our conversation.

"Well, it's almost time. Only a few more hours now," I said as lunch wound down. All I got in response from Mrs. Fraser was a huff. She scurried around the kitchen, clearing plates, cleaning dishes, packing food. I glanced at Mr. Fraser, who offered a weak smile and a slight shrug. A man of few words, Mr. Fraser's nervousness wasn't perceptible, but knowing him as I do, I realized he was just as on edge as the rest of us.

We gathered at the castle's front in the mid-afternoon. Mrs. Fraser stood straight as a board; her hands clasped in front of her. If I would have come upon her, I may have believed her a statue. Mr. Fraser passed the time admiring the scenery. I kicked a few stones around on the drive until I saw Mr. Smythe's sleek black rental car winding down the drive.

Suffice it to say, a myriad of thoughts raced through my brain as Mr. Smythe eased the car to a stop outside the castle's main entrance. I opened the door for Ms. Pearson, Mr. Smythe's secretary, and our newest Countess.

I began to unload the luggage as she climbed from the car. She stepped out and stared up at the castle. Her brunette hair fell just past her shoulders, framing her fair skin. She held a small black and white dog in her arms. She kissed the little guy on the top of his head and said, "We're home, Riley, we're home."

I probably realized then that I'd like her. She seemed kind, quiet, a gentle soul. What she said next made me certain we'd be friends. Mrs. Fraser began to discuss bedrooms for everyone and what she did with the boxes sent over from the new owner. That's when Lady Cate stepped forward. She extended her hand and simply said, "Hi, I'm Cate and this is Riley."

I'm surprised Mrs. Fraser didn't faint dead away at that

moment. She barely shook her hand she was in such shock. I stepped forward and gave her a good, strong handshake. "Good to meet ya, Cate," I answered her. "And a big hello to you, too, Sir Riley." I gave the little pooch a tickle under his chin. He seemed like an agreeable little fellow.

"Call me, Cate," she answered when Mrs. Fraser addressed her as Dr. Kensie. While Mrs. Fraser gasped at her "improper" behavior, I took her at her word. She seemed down-to-earth and friendly. She even offered to carry her luggage! We had a good laugh over her ability to handle that heavy bag but, in the end, I won that debate and carried her bags up for her. It would mark the first and last argument I'd ever win with her.

I delivered her luggage to her room, and we had a nice conversation about my off-the-cuff manner, which she didn't seem to mind. Lucky for me! I apologized for calling her Cate but said I took her at her word. My nerves played up after I said that, and I wondered if she'd give me the boot in short order. But the lassie didn't seem to mind one bit. After I was certain I'd remain employed, I left her to explore her new quarters with an extravagant bow, addressing her as "M'lady" which is now my nickname of choice for her.

I suppose the few brief conversations I'd had with Lady Cate set my mind at ease enough to sleep well that night. I quite liked her and didn't feel she'd cause too many waves at Dunhaven Castle. Mrs. Fraser wasn't as certain as I was.

The conversation in the kitchen the following morning would have had Lady Cate's ears burning had she overheard it.

"In the two-hundred-plus years of this castle standing tall on the hill, that woman is the worst thing to happen to it," Mrs. Fraser said as she bustled about the kitchen readying the meal for Lady Cate and her guests.

"Oh, Emily," Mr. Fraser chided, "let's give her a chance."

"Give her a chance, bah!" Mrs. Fraser retorted. "I'd like to give her something and it wouldn't be a chance! It would be a swift kick to her… "

"Emily!" Mr. Fraser interrupted before her language turned colorful.

She sighed as she prepared the oatmeal. "I cannae help it," she admitted. "I dinnae like it, I dinnae like it at all!"

"Give it some time," I counseled.

"I cannae believe that they could find no closer relative to Lady MacKenzie," Mrs. Fraser continued.

"Oh, I think she's a bit of all right," I answered.

"Call me Cate," Mrs. Fraser mimicked. "Now we've got a typical crass American running Dunhaven Castle. I say if Lady MacKenzie knew, she'd be turning in her grave."

"Ah, come on now, Mrs. Fraser," I answered. "She's not THAT bad and a bonnie lass if I ever saw one."

"Humph," Mrs. Fraser huffed at me, "she wouldn't know the first thing about being a lady. I can tell you that."

I raised my eyebrows at the statement. "I guess that depends on how you define a lady," I said

Mrs. Fraser snapped her head in the direction of the hallway leading up to the dining room.

"What is it, Emily?" Mr. Fraser questioned.

"Thought I heard something," Mrs. Fraser answered. She peered down the hall before shrugging. "I guess not. Anyway, time will tell, young Jack, time will tell."

Mrs. Fraser grasped the tureen of oatmeal and carried it from the room. I shot a glance to Mr. Fraser, who shrugged his shoulders. We were in for a rough couple of days and perhaps then some if Mrs. Fraser didn't warm up to Lady Cate.

I'm not certain how breakfast upstairs went, but downstairs we were as silent as church mice. The conversation before the meal dampened everyone's spirits a little, and we all remained on edge.

Afterward, Mr. Fraser and I headed out for the day to take care of our endless summer trimming and maintenance. Within an hour, though, Lady Cate called me back to the castle to help shuttle boxes from the library to her bedroom suite. An easy enough task, it didn't take me long to complete.

I stopped back in the kitchen afterward to snag another of Mrs. Fraser's famous shortbread biscuits. It surprised me to find Mrs. Fraser flitting around the kitchen as she hummed a tune under her breath.

"Well, your mood certainly seems to have improved," I said to her as she clicked her tongue at me for snatching a biscuit from her secret biscuit tin.

"You're about to turn it back around with your misbehavior," she scolded me.

I shot her a closed-mouth grin as I munched on the biscuit. "Come on, Mrs. Fraser," I prodded. "What's happened to brighten your day?"

Mrs. Fraser shrugged her shoulders at me as she dried a pot. "I may or may not be coming around to your way of thinking is all," she answered.

I raised my eyebrows at her. "Care to elaborate?" I questioned.

"Lady Cate... may not be as bad as I anticipated," she admitted.

My eyebrows raised further. "Lady Cate, is it?" I inquired.

Mrs. Fraser shot me a glance. "What?" I asked. "This morning you were ready to kick her in her…"

"Watch your mouth, young Jack," she interrupted me, "or I'll wash it out with soap."

"Your words, Mrs. Fraser. And now we've made it all the way to Lady Cate?"

"And that's as far as we're making it. I will NOT call her Cate," Mrs. Fraser said with a resolute nod.

I realized I'd likely not pry any additional information from Mrs. Fraser at the moment, but it was obvious something had shifted in her relationship with our newest Countess. I found out later that Lady Cate had spoken with Mrs. Fraser following her first breakfast in the castle. Not only had she assured Mrs. Fraser her job remained safe, but she had also informed her that she intended to make good on the late Lady MacKenzie's promise to bequeath their little cottage to them.

Cate's quick gesture to settle Mrs. Fraser's nerves went a long way to winning her over. Sure, she wasn't a stuffy blueblood, but she'd won Mrs. Fraser over with her kindness.

Mr. Smythe spent his time at the castle completing all the paperwork to finalize Lady Cate's takeover of the property. He gave a touching toast to her health after he concluded all aspects of the transfer. In true Lady Cate fashion, she insisted her staff join the toast and share in the moment.

Over the next few days, Ms. Pearson helped Cate settle into the castle. The little tyke she brought with her seemed to adjust easily. He loved bounding around the property, chasing after a little blue ball that Lady Cate tossed to him.

Lady Cate also seemed to be adjusting well. With all her unpacking done, she never seemed to tire of exploring her new home or the grounds. I often spotted her and Riley lounging by the loch and enjoying the scenery.

Everything appeared to be getting back to normal. Mr. and Mrs. Fraser were settled, as was I. We weren't losing our jobs (or our home, in the case of the Frasers). The new countess would prove to be as gracious as the last. We could all breathe a sigh of relief.

Of course, the adjustment wouldn't come without some hiccups. After Ms. Pearson returned to London, Lady Cate wandered into the kitchen while exploring the castle. Mrs. Fraser considered it a mistake, guessing Lady Cate had gotten herself lost. I'm not certain I've seen a more shocked expression on her face than I did that day. It may have even topped the expression when Lady Cate introduced herself as "just Cate."

When I waltzed through the door for lunch, I found Lady Cate seated at the table and a frazzled Mrs. Fraser putting the finishing touches on lunch. We'd never spotted Lady MacKenzie below stairs in her lifetime, not even if an issue existed. Odd to find our newest countess sitting at the "servant's table." After the initial shock wore off, everyone enjoyed the lunch. Lady Cate was determined to learn about her staff, and her interest seemed genuine. Dunhaven, it would seem, would move forward in a new direction!

Over the next few weeks, life settled down. Though differences still abounded at every turn. Lady Cate often appeared in the kitchen and carried her own meals upstairs. Though other than that, she kept to herself a good bit, not unlike her predecessor.

Not long after her arrival, Lady Cate inquired about a trip into town. Happy to oblige her, we settled on a day and I drove her into our tiny hamlet. The lassie wanted to visit the library, of all places, but promised me lunch at the pub.

This is where the story really takes off. Of course, we were all still completely oblivious to what lay ahead of us. In retrospect, this moment marked the turning point, though neither Cate nor I realized it.

It started small. The conversation seemed so innocent on the surface. As we lunched at the pub that day, Cate confessed she thought she'd broken a piece of her inheritance. The object in question was a gold pocket watch. As a small boy, I recalled Lady Gertrude MacKenzie, Cate's predecessor, wearing it as a pendant around her neck all the time. As we discussed my family's history with the estate, I made mention of that to Cate.

"Oh," Cate moaned as she grabbed the watch in her hand, "yes, apparently, it was important to her. She left me a handwritten note as part of the inheritance telling me I needed to wear it at all times. I thought it was odd, but I guess it was just really important to her."

"Must have been!" I responded.

"Which makes me feel even worse," Cate said with a sigh.

My brow furrowed as I tried to understand her meaning. What had the poor lassie so upset, I wondered?

"You lost me, Lady Cate, feel worse about what?"

"Oh, I think I may have broken the watch," she confessed.

I couldn't imagine how she could have broken it. "Oh, broken it? You Americans, riding roughshod over everything. How did you do that, drop it from the turret?" I inquired.

Cate shrugged and replied, "No idea. But it keeps slowing down, sometimes it seems almost to stop. Then it starts up again as if nothing was wrong. I need to have it looked at."

"My grandfather could take a look if you'd like. He's not a genuine watchmaker, but he's good with those kinds of things."

I explained my grandfather worked at Dunhaven Castle for Lady MacKenzie's mother, Mary. Lady Cate agreed, and we planned to stop on our way back to the castle after our lunch. We finished the conversation as our food arrived. Lady Cate ordered the fish and chips, claiming not to be adventurous. It would prove to be the start of a trend with her and about the least adventurous thing she'd do!

I learned a lot about Lady Cate over that enjoyable little lunch. Our newest countess had done little traveling outside of her home country before joining us on this side of the pond. She was about to make up for that in a major way!

On our way back to the castle, we stopped at my grandfather's cottage. Cate handed the timepiece to Pap after thanking him for agreeing to look at it.

"I can remember this watch from when I was a young man on the estate," Pap said.

"Oh, yes, Jack mentioned that you worked there. And his father, too," Cate answered.

"Aye, lassie, there's always been a Reid on that estate, it's tradition! Wouldn't seem right without us!" Pap answered.

"Well, I'm glad to have Jack there!"

I was glad to hear that comment!

"Now let me see the watch. Think you may have broken it, do you, lassie? Let me take a look."

Pap took the watch to his desk. A large magnifier was clamped onto the desk's side. Pap's jeweler's toolkit lay open across the desk. He took the jeweler's pliers and carefully opened the watch. He peered through the magnifying glass, eyeing the inside. He worked with the timepiece delicately. He seemed to hold almost a reverence for it. It struck me the way he treated the heirloom. Almost as though it was a Reid family heirloom rather than a MacKenzie one.

"Now, come on over here, Jackie," Pap said with a wave, "take a look at the inside and I'll show you some important parts."

Pap pointed out a few elements of the watch's inner workings as Cate explained the issue she experienced with the timepiece. I'd never seen the inside of a watch of this kind before. Well, to be honest, I'd never seen the inside of any watch. I wondered if they all worked the same way. I'd never remember everything he was telling me right now. I hoped to Google it later.

Cate answered, "Yes. I was telling Jack. It seems to slow suddenly, almost to a stop, and it seems to tick very loudly when it does that. Then, it will just start back up again like nothing was wrong."

"You hit the nail on the head with that last one, lassie!" Pap answered.

"I'm sorry, I don't understand, what did I do?" Cate inquired.

"You're right, nothing is wrong with it."

"Are you sure? It seems to slow almost to a stop, it's done it a few times, that can't be normal."

"I assure you, it's right as rain, this watch."

It looked okay to me. The little parts inside whirred without any trouble.

Seemed like Cate wasn't as certain. "I trust your experience, Mr. Reid, but would it still be prudent to have a watchmaker look at it, just to make sure it's in tip-top shape?"

"Nay, I'd not recommend that, lassie. Not at all." The suggestion surprised me as well, though not because I doubted my grandfather's assessment.

"Really? May I ask why?"

"It's quite an expensive piece, I'd not let it out of my sight. Lady MacKenzie was never without it, I'm sure that's why."

The explanation satisfied me. The heirloom must be worth quite a bit. Besides the threat of it being stolen, it could also become damaged.

"Did she ever have it serviced, I mean, that you know of?" Cate questioned.

"Nay, she never did. If anything needed fixing, I took care of it. She would have trusted no one else outside of the estate to care for the watch."

Good to know, I figured. I'd better study up. It would now be my responsibility to care for the timepiece.

"Hmm. That's interesting. Well, thanks so much for looking, I'm glad to know I haven't broken it, at least!"

"You're welcome, lassie, I'm happy to help."

"Well, we'll be on our way," Cate said.

My grandfather walked us to the door. I said goodbye to him, promising I'd be there for dinner on Sunday. I gave him a hug and a clap on the back. Cate thanked Pap again before leaving, and we returned to the car.

"Well," I said as we climbed into the car, "at least you've got the official word that you haven't broken it."

"Yeah, that's a relief. I've not ruined my inheritance just weeks in," Cate said with a laugh.

Despite the odd behavior Cate described, I figured it must be some tic (pun intended!) of the aging mechanism. I almost forgot about the timepiece's curious behavior, though Cate didn't. That would prove a growing trend. When Cate gets on to something, she's like a dog with a bone! That little tic would be the impetus for the entire chain of events to unfold. That little tic would change our lives.

CHAPTER 2

August 18
12:38 p.m.

It wasn't long before I'd hear from Cate again about that little tic. A few days later, Cate sent me a video via text message. In the video, she recorded the watch's odd performance. Not that I didn't believe her story, but this proved it beyond a doubt. The video showed the timepiece's second hand creeping along. If you didn't pay careful attention, it appeared as though the timepiece was completely stopped. Cate explained nothing changed the watch's behavior. Winding it, shaking it, tilting it, nothing altered the slowly ticking timepiece. She demonstrated all this in the video. The timepiece would eventually begin keeping normal time, seemingly without reason. In fact, during the video she sent, the watch began to speed and keep normal time after she swiped it to clear any fingerprints from the face.

THE SECRET KEEPERS: JACK'S JOURNAL #1

She requested I show the video to my grandfather. I could tell she wasn't convinced his assessment about the watch was correct.

I firmly believe in my grandfather's skills, but I promised to show him the video. I couldn't deny the behavior was odd. It did appear the timepiece was malfunctioning.

I stopped in at my grandfather's cottage the next day while on an errand run into town.

"Hey, Pap!" I called as I let myself in the front door.

"Jackie? That you?" he called from the kitchen.

"That it is," I answered.

He appeared in the doorway, wiping his hands with a towel. "I've got a question for you. You busy?" I asked.

He shrugged. "Nothing that can't wait, Jackie. Got time for a cuppa?"

"Sure," I answered. We stepped into the kitchen and Pap filled his tea kettle, setting it on the stove. I grabbed two mugs from the cupboard next to the sink and some cream from the refrigerator before settling at the table. In short order, the tea kettle announced teatime. Pap poured the steaming water into our mugs and plopped onto a chair across from me.

"So, what brings you by, Jackie?"

"What? I can't just want to drop in on my Pap?"

He offered me a smirk. "You said you had a question."

"Can't get anything past you."

"My memory hasn't gone yet! I'm not THAT old."

I chuckled as I pulled my phone from my pocket. "Cate sent me a video," I began.

"Cate, is it? Lady Kensie, you mean?"

"Lady Cate," I corrected with a glance to him. "Though she doesn't mind if we call her Cate."

He narrowed his eyes at me with a smirk on his face. "Don't give me that look, Pap." I tapped around on my phone and pulled up Cate's message. "Here's the video she sent." I played it. Cate's voice filled the air. She described the problem with the timepiece, and the video showed it slowing to a near stop. As the video wound down, the watch sped up, returning to its normal workings. I clicked my phone off as the movie stopped. "Any thoughts on that?"

Pap leaned back in his chair and crossed his arms. He jutted his lower lip out and shook his head. "Nay, laddie," he answered.

"Should she have it serviced? I mean, it's not working properly, is it? This proves it."

"It's working just fine, Jackie. It's just a tic of the thing." Pap stopped a moment to let out a large laugh and offered a wink before adding, "Pun intended."

I gave him a hearty laugh at his joke. "Just a tic, huh?"

He nodded. "Just a tic. Jackie, that timepiece is centuries old. Douglas MacKenzie himself had it made. She still keeps perfect time, I assure you. It's just an oddity of its aging."

I considered that statement as I took a sip of my tea. "You're sure?" I asked after a moment.

"Would I lie to you?" Pap answered.

"No," I said with a chuckle. "No, I suppose you wouldn't. I just want to reassure Lady Cate. She's convinced it's broken."

"Well, convince her it's not. Because it isn't. I promise that watch is working exactly as it was intended."

I nodded as I finished my tea. "Okay," I agreed. "I'll do my best. I don't know the lassie well, but she's got a mind of her own and I'm not certain I'm up to the task."

My grandfather's eyes grew to the size of saucers. "Better learn how or you'll have your work cut out for you."

"Well, she is the boss, so I suppose I shouldn't try to manage her."

"And you're her estate manager. An intricate part of the

workings of that estate. You'll need to have a good handle on how to convince her of what you feel is best."

"Well, I suppose for being headstrong, she's got a good head on her shoulders, so it shouldn't be too hard a task."

"Aye, she seems a right lassie," Pap agreed. "And it seems you two get along well so far."

I nodded in agreement. "I suppose we do. We hit it off straight away."

Pap grinned at me over his teacup. "Well, I'd better get going," I said. "I'll pass your message along to Lady Cate. Thanks, Pap."

"Anytime, Jackie. Pass my regards on to the lassie."

"Will do." I squeezed his shoulder before letting myself out.

I drove into town. Before I climbed from the car to head into the hardware store, I texted Lady Cate with the news. She responded with a "thanks." I'd bet she was less than enthused with the answer, but I trusted my grandfather's judgment.

In retrospect, he hadn't actually lied to me. The crafty bugger had worded it in just the right way so as not to blatantly lie but also not reveal the truth.

We let the matter drop, but it would resurface in two days. Cate texted me that afternoon with another tale about the watch. In this instance, a new twist arose. Cate described the same symptoms of the timepiece. She added that when the watch slowed, she also lost her cell service. She conjectured the two incidents were related.

The first thing that popped into my mind was some sort of electromagnetic pulse. I texted the idea back to her along with the promise to run the idea past my grandfather, too. We agreed to talk about it the following day.

My mind whirled through the possibilities as I continued my work that afternoon. An EMP didn't really fit the situation. Cate didn't mention anything else affected. And would the timepiece and the cell phone, two items separated by centuries of technology, share anything in common?

Nothing else occurred to me as a possible solution. I admit I remained extremely puzzled. When I finished my day, I joined my grandfather for dinner.

"Lady Cate's had another incident with her inheritance," I mentioned over our Scotch pie.

"Oh? Did you manage to convince her it's just an oddity with an aging device?"

"Not really," I admitted. "But she noticed a new anomaly."

"With the watch?"

"No, with her cell phone."

"What's her cell phone have to do with her watch?"

"That's the million-dollar question," I answered. "She says each time the timepiece slows, her cell phone loses its signal. She conjectures the two are related."

"I can't see how," Pap answered.

"Neither can I," I agreed. "My first idea was an EMP, but..." My voice trailed off while I processed my thoughts from earlier in the afternoon.

"The timepiece and cell phone don't share any parts in common," Pap finished for me.

"Right. And they likely don't even have anything in common that would be affected by that type of device."

"No," Pap agreed with a shake of his head. "The mechanisms running that timepiece wouldn't be affected by an EMP. The guts have never been updated to modern parts."

I nodded as I took another bite. "So, there goes that theory."

Pap nodded before changing the subject to discuss summer maintenance on the estate.

The next morning, Lady Cate and Sir Riley ran into me

on their morning walk as I trimmed a few shrubs at the edge of the property.

"Well, good morning to you, Cate, and to you, good Sir Riley!" I called over to them.

"Good morning," Cate greeted me. "How are you doing today?"

"Can't complain!" I answered. "I see we're coatless today, adjusting to our weather, are we?" I inquired, referencing her lack of coat. Poor Cate's previous residence enjoyed warmer weather than Dunhaven.

"Haha!" she laughed. "It's a bright sunny day, so I left the coat inside! So, did you talk to your grandfather about the watch?"

"Yes," I answered. "We couldn't come up with anything. The watch is old. He didn't think there were any parts the watch would have in common with a cell phone."

"I tried to look around on the Internet yesterday, but I saw nothing that made sense," Cate admitted with a shrug.

"Perhaps it was a coincidence?" I postulated.

"Possibly, but that's the second time it's happened and when I walked around I had no cell service even where I usually have it, that's the strange thing. And as soon as the watch started keeping normal time again, my service came back almost immediately," Cate explained.

"That is strange, but still, possibly a coincidence? I can't figure out anything that would affect both," I answered with a shrug. "Sorry, I don't have a better answer."

"It's okay," Cate said. "I don't either. Nothing makes sense, so maybe it is a coincidence. Maybe I'm reading more into it than there is."

Cate promised to keep me informed of any additional oddities that occurred with the watch. I reassured her about my grandfather's skills in estate matters. Before we parted ways, I brandished a branch for the little pup. His little brown eyes sparkled at the promise of the chase. I flung the stick away and said goodbye to Lady Cate before returning to trimming. I do like that little pup.

We wouldn't have to wait long for another incident. Cate texted me the next morning stating she had a theory and requested a lunch meeting. Unfortunately, I was running errands in town, so I had to decline. But as luck would have it, Lady Cate was also heading to town. She offered to meet for lunch at the pub, which I accepted without hesitation. We planned for noon.

I arrived at the pub first and slid into a booth across from the entrance. When Cate arrived, she thanked me for meeting her as she sat down across from me.

"Thanks for meeting me," she said. "Riley says hi."

"No problem, I'm dying to hear your theory about the watch," I answered. What had Cate discovered, I wondered? "Oh, and tell the little lad I say hello, too, and I look forward to another game of fetch real soon."

The arrival of the waitress postponed any further conversation. As the lassie left with our order, I commented on Cate's choice. "Fish and chips again? Really?"

"It's good and I'm not very adventurous, I guess," Cate answered.

I let out a hearty laugh at that remark. "Oh, right, this coming from the lassie who moved to a new country and castle sight unseen."

"Not true! Mr. Smythe showed me pictures," Cate joked back, "so I saw it." She offered me a wry glance.

"Ah, you're right, not very adventurous moving to a new country when you saw pictures." I laughed again. Then my curiosity got the better of me. "Okay, down to business, what's your theory on the watch?"

"One word: friction." Cate grinned at me.

I had no idea what she meant. "Friction? Care to elaborate?"

"Yes, friction," she explained, "I've developed this kind of habit of rubbing the watch in my hand. I think the friction from my hand may affect it. It happened again last night, just after I was rubbing the watch. When I thought back, I think every time it's happened it has been when I've been handling the watch like that. Here, let me show you."

Cate grabbed the watch and began rubbing it. Nothing happened. She frowned and tried again. But again, it produced no result. She sighed, sounding disgusted. "This is what I was doing last night and when I rubbed it again, the watch sped up and went back to perfect time."

"Are you sure it wasn't just a coincidence?" I inquired.

"I thought of that but, from what I remember, it's typically happened when I've been rubbing the watch."

"Except now," I pointed out.

"Except now, yes," she murmured as she tried rubbing the watch again. "Except now."

"I'll run it past my grandfather and see what he says. Assuming, though, that you've got something here, like maybe it worked last night because it built up all day with friction, how does that explain the cell phone signal loss?"

"That's the only piece that doesn't fit into this scenario, I don't know. But maybe I'm on to something, even if this isn't exactly it. You could be right; maybe it's a buildup. Although, it's happened earlier in the day, too, so that wouldn't fit well there," Cate answered.

"Well," I said as the waitress returned with our food, "perhaps we're moving in the right direction. Keep tabs on it, for now though, let's enjoy our meal."

We finished our lunch, avoiding the subject of the watch. I had no solutions for Lady Cate. My grandfather assured me no issue existed with the timepiece. Yet Cate insisted the problem persisted. It's not that I didn't believe her, but what could be causing it? And was it anything to be concerned about? I trusted my grandfather's judgment but understood Lady Cate's concern. Perhaps time would tell, I figured, pun definitely intended.

The next day, the issue with the watch took another odd turn. I trimmed rose bushes in the back garden when a frenzied knock sounded from a window above me.

I searched the windows and found one open with Cate framed inside.

"M'lady!" I shouted, giving her an exaggerated bow. "Why doth though beckon from the window?"

At least my bad jokes made Lady Cate laugh. She shook her head at me as she chuckled before she answered, "Very funny. I beckon from the window because I've been looking for you."

"That sounds ominous," I answered.

"Did you just get here? I went past here earlier and didn't see you. That thing happened with the watch again, I wanted to show you."

"I've been here for over two hours. And I can tell you it's true: every rose really does have its thorn. Maybe even two or three of them!"

Even at a distance, I could read the confusion on Cate's face. "Everything okay, Cate?" I inquired.

"Ah, yes, I think so, it's just that, well, I just came past, and I could have sworn you were not here."

Now it was my turn to be confused. I hadn't moved from that spot in hours. "I promise I've been here for about two hours, haven't left."

"No, I believe you, but I'm surprised I could have missed you. Hey, speaking of working, did Mr. Fraser hire some extra help for the garden trimming?"

"Extra help?" The confusion multiplied. We never hired extra help for trimming.

"Yes, I saw a man a few yards down working outside the garden, I was wondering who he was."

"Ah." I hesitated, uncertain how to answer. Cate insisted she saw someone, yet I knew no one else was working on the estate. "There's no one else working with us today that I know of. If he hired someone, he didn't mention it to me, and I haven't seen anyone all day." I didn't want to insult her. And I didn't disbelieve her, yet there was no way it could be true.

Cate shouted back, "Hmmm, well, anyway, we can chat later about it. I'll let you get back to your roses!"

"I believe they're YOUR roses, Lady Cate." I saluted her before returning to my work. As I trimmed the bushes, the conversation replayed in my mind. Lady Cate's frantic knock suggested something portentous. While she mentioned the timepiece's odd behavior, the focus of the conversation ended up being a strange man Cate saw on the estate.

No one else was on the estate working outside. While I trusted Cate's encounter was real, I couldn't imagine who it could have been. After I cleaned up my rose trimmings and collected my tools, I took a stroll down the length of the castle. I searched for any evidence of the man Cate spoke of but found none. Not even a broken branch on the ground betrayed any evidence of his existence.

I put it out of my mind as I returned home that night. I chalked it up to the new environment and a trick of the mind.

The next day, though, I wouldn't be able to explain it away so easily. As I tended an ailing rose bush, Cate and Riley greeted me.

I said hello to both of them, giving Riley a pat on his head.

"You don't look happy," Cate said.

"I'm not. This little lad doesn't seem to be doing so well." I pointed out a few of the shriveled leaves. "I was trying to determine what might be wrong with it. I might have to call in reinforcements, my grandfather might have a better idea than I."

"Oh, speaking of," Cate answered, "I was hoping to interview him for my book. Since he's lived here and worked on the estate, I think he would have a great wealth of knowledge about it. If he's coming to look at the rose bush, would you mind asking him for me?"

Pap would love that, I figured. "Ah, I'm sure he'd be happy to talk for as long as you'd like about the castle. Maybe even longer than you'd like," I answered with a laugh. "He's probably got loads of information to share. He's out of town, so I'll ask as soon as he's back."

"I'll bet, that's why he's a perfect source for my book."

I decided to follow up on the man Cate spotted yesterday. The encounter remained on my mind despite my best ability to shake it. "Say, speaking of people at the castle, did you track down that extra helper you saw yesterday?"

"Uh, no," Cate said with a frown.

"Now you don't look happy, Cate." Had she realized he didn't exist or was there something else, I wondered?

Cate hesitated. She stared down at Riley, a pensive expression on her face. What was she thinking? I prodded a little more. "Cate, is everything okay?"

"I think so," she answered with a shrug.

"You think so? You don't sound so sure."

Again, she paused for a moment, her attention focused on the little dog. "It's just that this is the second person I've seen on this estate that no one else has seen and when no one else has been on the property other than you, me and the

Frasers."

Her admission stunned me. "The second time?"

"Yes," Cate admitted, "I saw a woman in the entry hall. I spoke to her, but Mrs. Fraser said there was no one else in the place when I asked her about it."

"Hmm," I mumbled as I processed the information. This added a new wrinkle. Two strange encounters on the estate? She must be mistaken. We'd never had problems with vagrants in the past. I didn't doubt her story, but I assumed it may be part of an overactive imagination due to the large life change.

Cate mistook my hesitance for disbelief on my part. "I'm not crazy. And I didn't think I believed in ghosts, but I'm wondering about those tales floating around town about this place."

"I don't think you're crazy, Cate. And I certainly don't believe those tales from town. Those people like to talk, that's all. It's Scotland, everyone's got a haunted something or other in their back pocket around here. It's just idle chatter, don't let it get in your head."

"But then how do you explain what I saw? If it's not ghosts, am I going crazy? What other explanation is there?"

"Cate," I said, putting my hands on her shoulders, "you've just moved from another country into a giant castle. I'm sure your nerves are on edge and your imagination is just playing tricks on you. You're primed to see something."

Cate didn't look convinced, but she gave in. "You're right, it's probably an overactive imagination combined with the unfamiliar setting. Plus, it can be kind of spooky here at night."

"Yeah, I'll bet, but I wouldn't know for sure, I'm too afraid to be here at night," I joked.

"Funny. You should be afraid during the day, that's when I

see all my ghosts." Cate laughed. "Well, time to get Riley his dinner. I'll leave you to your sick rose, I hope it's okay!"

"Okay, Cate. Enjoy your dinner, Sir Riley!"

As I switched on my TV later that evening, my mind wandered back to my discussion with Cate. What was going on? Cate seemed stable with a good head on her shoulders. I told her she was imagining things. But I was starting to question my own explanation. Would Lady Cate really imagine not one, but two people on the estate? Even a trick of the mind seemed a stretch. For it to happen twice seemed less than probable.

Cate described seeing a woman in the foyer. She spoke to her. That couldn't have been a figment of her imagination. Would she really speak with someone she wasn't sure was there?

Questions piled up faster than I could process them. And no answers were forthcoming. A problem with the timepiece that was apparently working properly, according to my grandfather. Not one, but two strangers spotted on the estate. What was going on?

I went to bed with no answers or theories. The next day would provide yet another incident that would advance us another step toward the most incredible discovery of our lives.

CHAPTER 3

August 18
3:23 p.m.

As I worked in the gardens the next morning, a little rascal called Riley raced toward me. I grabbed one of the sticks I'd pulled from the hedge and Riley bit the other end. He tugged on it ferociously. He had quite a grip for such a little guy!

A moment later, Cate rounded the corner. "Ah, good morning, Cate! I thought Sir Riley had let himself out for a walk."

"No, he's faster at dodging bushes than I am," Cate said with a chuckle.

"I'll bet he is, and he's not too shabby at tug of war either. He's got quite a grip, this little one has." Riley managed to tug the branch away from me. He trotted to Cate with his bounty. "You win, big guy, you win," I told him before turning to speak to Cate. "And how are you today?"

"I'm fine."

The brief response made me wonder if she really was fine. "Haven't seen any ghosts today, have you?" I teased.

"No, I haven't seen any ghosts today, thank you," she said with a coy glance. "BUT I made the watch slow down AND speed up. It has to have something to do with friction!"

"Rubbing it? But that didn't work the last time," I reminded her.

"No, but it did this morning. It can't be a coincidence."

"Try it again," I suggested, prompting her to try the trick now.

"Okay." I glanced over Cate's shoulder as she rubbed the watch. Nothing happened. Cate frowned at it. "Come on, you!" she said to it.

"Talking to watches? NOW, I think you're crazy, Cate," I joked.

"It just worked!" She tried it two more times, but the timepiece did not slow. "It wasn't over two hours ago! This is so frustrating!"

"Maybe it doesn't like me, maybe it's shy. Did you lose your cell signal again when it happened?" I inquired.

"I don't know. I didn't check," Cate admitted. "I thought I heard Mrs. Fraser talking in the hall, so I got the watch back up to speed and went to check."

"What did she want?" I questioned.

"Nothing, she wasn't there. When I asked her about it this morning, she said she wasn't in the castle."

My brow furrowed. Worry built as I considered the new information. Cate seemed to be a level-headed woman. I doubted she could concoct another imagined event. Nor did I expect she'd broadcast it if she wasn't certain.

"I'm NOT crazy," Cate answered my confused expression.

"I didn't say you were, I'm a little concerned that someone might have been in the castle," I admitted.

"Who would have been there and why?" Cate asked.

"That's the million-dollar question. Whoever it may have been, I can't imagine they were up to anything good at 5:30 a.m. in someone else's home."

"Okay, that's creepy on a different level, but that would make sense with some things I've been experiencing. But again, why?"

"I can come up with a million reasons: a free place to live, hiding out from someone, trying to scare the new owner. Who knows? But I'm getting concerned that maybe it's not your overactive imagination and your big move that is the cause here."

"Do you think I should call the police?"

We weren't there yet, but I was concerned enough to want to search the castle. "We don't have proof of anything. Do you mind if I look around?"

"Not at all. I'd feel better if you did, in fact. And I'd like to help! I want to see with my own eyes that no one is here."

"Okay, let's check it out, top to bottom, if your ghost is in there and alive, we'll find 'em."

We spent the next few hours searching the castle. We found nothing in the servant's area, nothing on the main floor, and next to nothing upstairs. But as we finished our search, well… I sometimes still can't believe this story. I've been over it again and again in my mind, detail by detail, and still, as I put it in black and white, I wonder if I imagined it.

With one bedroom remaining and nothing found so far, Cate was ready to give up. She informed me she'd spent a fair amount of time in the room. Apparently, she'd found trunks filled with old clothes and love letters and had been in and out of the room often. I suggested we check it out just to be safe. With a shrug, Cate agreed.

I searched the main bedroom while Cate ducked into the closet. "I don't see anything," she shouted from inside, "but this is one place this watch loves to do its trick! Maybe it'll work here, and you can finally see it!"

"Okay!" I shouted back. I waited a moment as I finished my brief search around the room. "Anything?" I called.

No one answered me. "Cate?" I yelled. No response. "Cate?" I strode to the closet. I glanced inside and found it empty. Where was Cate hiding? Did she step out of the room? Little Riley stood behind me, glancing up at me with a quizzical expression on his tiny black and white face. Wherever Lady Cate went, she didn't take Riley. Odd, I mused.

I stepped out of the closet and pulled open the bedroom door. I glanced up and down the hallway, finding nothing. I shook my head and returned to the room. I must have missed Cate. I marched back to the closet.

As I stepped through the doorway, Cate and I collided. She stumbled back a step, and I grabbed her before she toppled over. What had happened, I wondered? Where had she been? Why hadn't she answered?

"Cate, where have you been?" I asked.

Her response puzzled me. "Where have I been?" she questioned. "Where have YOU been?" She raised her eyebrows at me as though I'd not been answering her.

My forehead wrinkled as I pondered her statement. "I've been right here the whole time. I called and called for you, but you didn't answer. I looked in the closet and you weren't here."

Cate's brows knit as I told her this. "I heard nothing. I called and called for YOU and you didn't answer. I looked in the room and back in here and neither you nor Riley were here!"

It made no sense. What was she saying? She wasn't in the closet, the bedroom or the hallway. I was certain of that. Yet, according to Cate's version, I was the one missing from all those places.

We stood in silence for a moment, both of us trying to make sense of what had just happened. Cate spoke first. "Do me a favor," she said. "I'd like to test something. Go out and close the door, wait about ten seconds, then open it and see if I'm here. Close the door and wait another few seconds, then open it again."

My mind struggled to wrap around her request. The confusion must have been apparent on my face. "Cate, what are you talking about?" I managed.

"Just trust me, try it," Cate answered.

"You're the boss," I said with a shrug.

Cate took a few steps backward into the closet. I stepped out and closed the door. I studied my watch as the seconds ticked by. After ten seconds, I opened the door. "Cate?" I called into the empty room. I searched the space. My brow furrowed as I found no one. My stomach began to feel a bit uneasy. Where in the world was Cate going? As instructed, I closed the door and waited another ten seconds. In the short amount of time, I pondered what might be going on.

"Where in the world did your owner go, Sir Riley?" I asked the small dog at my feet.

When the ten seconds passed, I pulled the door open. In the middle of the room stood Cate. She appeared nervous and said, "Please tell me this is the first time you've opened that door."

"This is the second time I've opened the door. The first time you weren't here. Cate, where did you go? Is there a secret passage in here?" I glanced around the space, searching for some indication of one.

Cate hesitated a moment before responding. "I don't know where I went, but I think it has something to do with this watch."

Her statements confounded me. I couldn't make sense of any of this, let alone her reaction to it. "You don't know where you went?" I asked. What did she mean by that? How could she not know where she went? "What could it possibly have to do with the watch?" How was the timepiece connected to this?

"I was standing here in the closet, but the door never opened," Cate explained. "I heard voices, I assumed it was you and opened the door myself, but no one was there. I walked all over searching for you and Riley but couldn't find you."

"What?" I asked with a laugh. I understood now. My new employer was pulling one over on me. "Cate, are you playing a prank on me? Come on, where is the secret passage or secret panel?"

"I'm not joking," Cate answered. "I wish there was a secret passage or whatever, but there isn't. Or if there is, I'm not aware of it. You were not here!"

"Cate, I can't believe that," I said. I hadn't moved, neither had Riley. We were right here the entire time. I couldn't understand anything she was saying.

"I'm not sure I want to believe it either, but it's the truth. I didn't see you, and the only thing that changed was this watch's speed."

My mind raced but still couldn't grasp anything meaningful. I paused as I gathered my thoughts, though I wasn't sure if I could make any sense of anything. "I don't know what to say. I can't think of a relevant question to even ask. I don't understand any of this," I admitted.

"Me either," Cate admitted. "But I can think of one question to ask."

"What's that?" I asked, staring at her.

"If you didn't see me here... where was I?"

"None of this makes any sense to me, Cate," I answered. "If you never left, where were you? Because you definitely weren't here!"

Cate sunk onto one of the trunks. The poor lassie looked a little green around the gills. "None of it makes any sense, you're right. Are you sure you didn't miss me?"

"Cate, there's no missing you. You're standing here plain as day in front of me. I didn't miss you."

"Possibly there is some mechanism that moves this closet?" Cate suggested, phrasing it as a question. "Perhaps there is a secret passage or panel that we aren't aware of that interacts with the watch."

"Okay," I said, vetting the idea. "But the closet looked the same just minus you. So, an identical space must be replacing it. And if it were moving, what mechanism is that quiet that no one would hear it? And how could the watch control it?"

Questions spilled directly from my mind to my mouth. I hadn't heard a thing, no whirring sound, no clanking, nothing to suggest a moving room.

"I don't know," Cate admitted. "But something strange is going on."

"That's the only thing we know for sure. Something strange is going on. Damn!" I exclaimed. "A fine time for my grandfather to be traveling. He'd be the perfect person to ask." If this room held a secret, Pap would know. He could clear this up easily!

I glanced down at Cate. The poor lassie appeared worse. "Cate, are you okay? You're white as a sheet."

"Yeah," Cate answered in a shaky voice. "Well, I mean, other than me disappearing with no explanation, I'm okay. I just don't know what to think anymore."

That uneasy feeling crept back into my belly. Something strange was happening here, and I didn't like it. "Until we know what to think, it might be best that you're not fiddling with this watch. We don't want you disappearing for good."

"Maybe you're right. We don't understand what it's doing or where I'm going, maybe I shouldn't mess with it."

"I'm not even sure you should keep coming to this closet. It may be something similar to what you suggested earlier being triggered by something we don't know of."

"Good point," Cate agreed. She stood from the trunk but sunk right back down.

"Whoa, you okay, Cate?" I asked as she collapsed.

"Yes," she assured me. "Just a little woozy. I think I'm letting my fear of the unknown get to me a little too much. I'm sure there's a reasonable explanation for this."

I couldn't offer any explanation, reasonable or otherwise. The only thing I could suggest was for Cate to lay down and get some rest. I offered to help her to her room. I was glad I did. She could barely stand let alone walk. Poor lassie. She recovered a bit as we approached her room. Poor little Riley followed us, concern written on his furry little face.

I told Cate I'd have Mrs. Fraser bring her lunch up. Before I left, I assured Cate we'd find that reasonable explanation. As I ducked from the room, I wondered if I could make good on my promise.

Nothing made sense. I replayed the encounter over and over in my mind as I traversed the halls. Had I missed Cate when I opened the door the first time? No, I resolved. I hadn't missed her. Just like I hadn't missed her the first time I searched the closet. She was gone. But where?

Did the moving room idea make sense? Surely, I would have heard the mechanism. Even if the mechanism was silent, wouldn't Cate feel the motion if the room was moving? That idea didn't make sense.

But if that idea didn't make sense, what did? Where had Cate gone?

I arrived at the kitchen, my mind still reeling. As usual, Mrs. Fraser didn't miss a trick.

"What's got that look on your face, young Jack?" she inquired.

I wasn't about to admit Cate's disappearing act to Mrs. Fraser. I was certain she'd assume I'd lost my marbles. While part of my worry stemmed from Cate's disappearance, the other arose from Cate's reaction to it.

"It's Lady Cate," I said.

"What about Lady Cate?" Mrs. Fraser inquired as she bustled around the kitchen.

"She's sick," I choked out.

Mrs. Fraser halted mid-step. "Sick? What?"

I swallowed hard, trying to gather myself for the conversation. "Yes," I said with a nod as I leaned against the counter for support. "She told me about her recent encounters on the estate."

"With the girl she saw in the foyer, you mean?"

I nodded. "Yes. And a man she spotted on the estate a few days ago. And then she said she heard a woman's voice early this morning. She assumed it was you but when she searched you weren't there and later said you weren't in the castle at that time."

"Aye, that's right. She asked me about it," Mrs. Fraser confirmed.

"It made me a tad worried someone may be on the estate," I answered.

"What? Who? And why?" Mrs. Fraser questioned.

"I have no idea, though, with three encounters, I worried someone may be. So, we searched the castle, top to bottom."

"And?" Mrs. Fraser said as she stirred a large stockpot on the stove.

"We found nothing," I admitted. "Lady Cate began to question what was going on," I fibbed. "She was certain she didn't imagine any of these incidents. I think she let her imagination of what might be happening run away with her."

"Poor girl," Mrs. Fraser answered. "The move has hit her hard. I'm sure it's difficult adjusting to a place this size. It's got all sorts of noises and quirks. Plus, if she's not feeling well, that's likely the reason."

I nodded.

Mrs. Fraser glanced up at me. "What is it? You still look terrible!"

I shrugged. "Poor Lady Cate was so awfully pale. I walked her back to her bedroom, and she could barely stand. I'm a bit worried about her still."

"Ah," Mrs. Fraser answered with a knowing smile. "Don't worry your little head over it. I'm making a batch of my famous chicken soup. It'll have Lady Cate right as rain in no time."

"I hope she gets some rest," I said.

"She will," Mrs. Fraser assured me. "I'll see to that. She won't move out of that bed until she's recovered!"

Mrs. Fraser ladled a large bowl of soup and positioned it on a tray. She spread an array of crackers on the underplate. Before she carried the tray up, Mrs. Fraser retrieved a bone for Riley. She wrapped it in a towel and set it on the tray before lifting it and carrying it away.

I meandered to the pot and took a whiff. I glanced at the oven top, spotting a fresh batch of biscuits still sitting on their baking sheet.

"Don't touch those biscuits before lunch!" Mrs. Fraser shouted down the hall. I grimaced and glanced around, wondering if Mrs. Fraser had cameras to spy on me.

With no biscuits to distract me, I returned to my worry for Lady Cate. I hadn't told Mrs. Fraser the truth about Cate's illness. It was far more involved than I let on. What caused it? What happened to Cate?

I wouldn't have time to ponder it much further. Mr. Fraser joined me, ready for a piping hot bowl of Mrs. Fraser's famous chicken soup. In short order, Mrs. Fraser returned. I have to admit, Mrs. Fraser's chicken soup is really the best I've ever eaten. Even better than Pap's, but don't tell him that.

After lunch, Mrs. Fraser checked on Cate. I nibbled on a few biscuits as I waited for her to return with a report on Lady Cate. She returned with a huff and an empty tray.

"Well?" I inquired with a mouthful of biscuit.

Mrs. Fraser removed a few biscuits from the baking sheet and placed them on a plate. "Lady Cate needs a few things," she answered. "I caught her climbing out of her bed to get them. I put her right back into it and told her you'd bring her everything she needs."

"Sure," I said as I stood.

"She requested her laptop, and a folder marked 'Castle research.' She said you'd find them both in the library. She's also earned herself a plate of biscuits. She ate all the soup just as I told her."

"Lucky Lady Cate," I said as I accepted the plate of biscuits. "Okay, laptop and castle research folder. Got it."

"And dinnae you eat any of those biscuits on the way up to Lady Cate's bedroom!" Mrs. Fraser shouted as I disappeared from the kitchen.

"I wouldn't dream of it, Mrs. Fraser!" I assured her. I glanced down at the plate. Four biscuits. Would Lady Cate notice if I only delivered three? I'd better not. Mrs. Fraser would know. I didn't understand how, but Mrs. Fraser would know.

I retrieved all the requested items and delivered them to Lady Cate. Cate and I had a short conversation as I dropped off her materials. I assured her we'd solve the problem and reiterated Mrs. Fraser's orders for her to rest.

She appeared much better. The color had returned to her face and her spirits seemed to have improved. That relieved a large part of my worry. Though the questions still lingered in my mind. Little did I know at the time how staggering the answers would be when we discovered them.

I finished my afternoon's work and returned to the castle for dinner. Mr. and Mrs. Fraser were in the kitchen engaged in a discussion when I arrived.

"Well, there he is now. I suppose we can ask him and finish our plans," Mrs. Fraser said.

"Uh-oh," I murmured. "Ask me what?"

"Ask you more about the situation with Lady Cate. But first I've got to get this food upstairs while it's still hot!"

Mrs. Fraser darted from the kitchen with her tray in hand. From the appearance of her meal, Mrs. Fraser placed Cate fully into the "sick" category. I hoped Cate had improved. Mrs. Fraser returned a few moments later with little Riley in her arms.

"On dog duty?" I inquired.

"Lady Cate is not to move from her bed. And little Riley needs his walking and his dinner!"

I lifted the little guy from Mrs. Fraser's arms. "I'll walk him," I said. "I had better use the leash, though. I'm not sure he'll listen to me as well as he listens to Lady Cate."

"Aye," Mrs. Fraser agreed. "And the last thing Lady Cate needs is to worry herself silly over the little pup. She keeps the leash and harness over here." Mrs. Fraser handed the items to me from a hook near the kitchen door.

In a few moments, I had Riley ready to go. We enjoyed a walk through the back garden before returning to the kitchen. Mrs. Fraser had his bowl filled and waiting, and the little laddie dug right in as Mrs. Fraser put the final touches on our meal. As we sat down to eat, Riley stretched himself near the warm oven for an after-dinner nap.

"Now, what's all this about Lady Cate's condition?" I inquired. "Is she worse?"

"Nay, no worse. And insisting she's just fine at every

opportunity but I feel uncomfortable leaving her in her condition and even more so after you searched the castle for an intruder. I propose we stay here tonight in case Lady Cate should need us."

"I don't disagree, Emily," Mr. Fraser chimed in. "But I dinnae want Lady Cate uncomfortable with us pushing ourselves in."

"Bah," I said with a wave of my hand, "Lady Cate wouldn't think that about either of you. And I agree with Mrs. Fraser. I wouldn't mind staying overnight either. I'm more than concerned about someone being in this place. Cate has had three strange encounters. I cannot believe she's imagining them."

"As strange as I find it that someone would be lurking around this castle, I agree. This cannae be a figment of Lady Cate's imagination," Mrs. Fraser said.

All eyes turned to Mr. Fraser. He held his hands up and nodded his head. "I prefer to be safe, not sorry. I just dinnae want Lady Cate to wish she wouldn't have promised us our jobs until retirement."

"Nay," I answered, "Lady Cate would not think that."

"Then it's settled. I'll tell Lady Cate when I retrieve her tray that we will all stay the night."

"Sounds fine to me. I can pick up anything you need from your cottage when I run home if you'd like."

"Nay, don't trouble yourself, young Jack," Mrs. Fraser answered. "I'll stay here with Lady Cate while you two men do the running."

"All right," I agreed. "I won't be long."

I collected my dinner dishes and delivered them to the sink.

"I'll have all the rooms made up before you're both back," Mrs. Fraser promised. "We'll stay in the same wing as Lady Cate."

"Okay," I agreed. "I'll be back soon!"

Mr. Fraser and I left the estate, each heading to our respective homes to collect our things. While the move did little to answer any of my questions, it brought me some measure of comfort. At least I felt like I was doing something, even if it wouldn't lead to any answers.

When I returned to the castle, Mrs. Fraser reported that Lady Cate was settled in bed for the night with little Riley at her side. She'd been appreciative that we were staying, though she had insisted she didn't want to put anyone out. Typical Cate, I reflected.

Mrs. Fraser had prepared a bedroom for me down the hall from Cate's suite and next door to the bedroom she and Mr. Fraser would stay in overnight. As I pulled the sheets over me, I listened for even the slightest noise. I strained hard so I wouldn't miss anything in case someone was lurking around the estate.

I glanced at the clock twenty minutes later. I was in for a long, sleepless night. I tossed and turned in my bed. The luxuriously comfortable mattress and sheets should have been everything I needed to drift off to the best night's sleep I'd had in my life, but I couldn't relax.

Each time I closed my eyes, visions of strange characters lurking around the property shot through my mind. After ninety minutes, I climbed out of bed and paced the floor of the oversized bedroom.

I stalked to the door and pressed my ear against it, listening. After a few moments, I cracked the door and peered into the darkened hallway. I saw nothing suspicious.

I eased the door shut and returned to pacing. After another few moments, I settled in front of the large window overlooking the property. I scanned the area visible from my room. Moonlight cast an eerie aura across the trees and shrubs, though I saw nothing moving and no evidence of anyone prowling around the grounds.

I returned to bed. For another hour, I laid staring at the bedroom's ornate ceiling. With a sigh, I threw the covers off and crawled from the bed. I padded across the room and eased open the door. I winced as it creaked a bit. I'd have to get some oil on that in the morning.

I squinted into the darkness filling the hallway. All appeared quiet. I crept a few steps out of the bedroom and glanced up and down the hall. Nothing stirred. I caught sight of Lady Cate's bedroom and wondered if she was having better luck sleeping.

I swung my head in the opposite direction. Now would be a perfect time to explore the castle. If someone was hiding here (and doing a fantastic job at covering their presence), I could catch them red-handed wherever they were holed up!

With a plan formed in my mind, I padded down the hall. I began checking bedrooms as I went. I flicked the lights on in every room, trying to make a quick but thorough search of each space.

I worked my way through the entire top floor. As I entered the bedroom with the trick closet, I paused. Where had Cate gone earlier when she'd disappeared? A knot formed in my stomach as the questions flooded back into my mind. Even if Cate's encounters with people on the estate could be explained by a squatter, how could we explain Cate's disappearing act?

I took a few moments to scrutinize the space. I felt around the doorway leading to the closet for any triggers. I glanced inside. I wasn't sure I wanted to enter the closet area, afraid I might disappear.

"You're being silly, old man," I chided myself. With a shaky breath, I stepped inside and scanned the place. Various trunks were scattered around, and a full-length mirror stood in the corner. I checked around the space, searching for any source of Cate's odd disappearance. I frowned as the closet provided no additional information for me.

I'll admit, I hurried out of it as soon as I finished my search. With a final glance at the room and no new answers, I switched off the lights and moved on. A search of the entire upstairs turned up nothing.

I moved to the main floor where, after a check of each room, I also came up empty. I headed below stairs. I ended my fruitless search in the kitchen. I wasn't certain if I felt better or worse that my midnight roamings had turned up nothing. No one was lurking around in the castle, but how did that explain Cate's sightings?

Before heading back to my room, I figured I'd earned a biscuit. I retrieved the tin Mrs. Fraser kept hidden on a top shelf in the kitchen and snagged two biscuits from it. I bit into one as I returned the tin. Mrs. Fraser baked one mean shortbread.

I finished the biscuits as I traversed the darkened halls back to my bedroom. I'd solved nothing. But I had gotten two biscuits, so I figured I'd come out on top. Perhaps now I could sleep. I crawled into bed and finally drifted off.

The next morning, Lady Cate joined us for breakfast. She appeared to be fully recovered. Everyone avoided anything beyond light conversation over the meal. I hoped to catch Cate alone later in the day to discuss things in private. As breakfast wound down, Mr. Fraser and I headed outside to begin our tasks for the day.

Within a few hours, Lady Cate approached from the path leading to the loch. She carried Riley in her arms. "Good morning, again," she yelled.

"Good morning, again. And what do we have here? Sir Riley too tired to walk?"

"I'm afraid I tired him out playing ball this morning."

"I'd have thought he'd have you tired out after your sleepless night. For what it's worth, I heard nothing last night." I didn't mention my walkabout through the castle. I didn't want to upset poor Cate more than she already was.

"Neither did I," Cate began. "I'm not surprised though. I think all those incidents are connected to the watch. I made some notes this morning and, if I'm correct, I encountered people on the property when the watch was slow. I tried it again this morning out here by the loch, but it didn't react. So that's the third time that I've tried the watch outside of the castle and it hasn't slowed, so I'd say that means that it only works in the castle itself. What it's doing I don't know, but…"

I interrupted her mid-sentence. "You tried it again this morning? I thought we agreed that you wouldn't mess around with that until we learned more about it."

Cate frowned at me. "How are we going to learn anything about it unless we test it?"

"Cate, this is not a good idea until we determine what's going on, which may never happen. But yesterday, you disappeared. You were not there. It's not wise to keep fooling around with something so strange. What if you get trapped somewhere and we can't find you?"

"Well, I hope we have some answers soon," Cate said, dodging my question.

"Me too," I agreed. "Until then, do nothing."

"Well, I better be heading back. I'll talk to you later!" Cate headed towards the castle.

It was an abrupt end to the conversation. I assumed Cate hadn't cared for my assessment of the situation. Perhaps I came across as preachy but I worried about messing around with something we knew so little about. Now the lassie was likely mad at me but if something happened to her, I'd have never forgiven myself for not saying something.

Cate avoided me for the rest of the day. At least, that's what I assumed. During dinner, Mrs. Fraser informed us there was no need to stay overnight. Lady Cate seemed fully recovered and discussed the matter with her.

Hmm, I wondered, was Cate upset with me? I grabbed my phone while we ate, risking the wrath of Emily Fraser, and sent a quick text to Cate: *u ok? Mrs. F said you didn't need us to stay, r u sure?*

Cate answered within moments: *I'm sure. I don't think anyone is on the property, I should be fine! Thanks!*

Well, she answered. Was she still sore at me about the lecture I'd given her? Or perhaps she merely did feel safer. I couldn't disagree with her. I'd found no evidence of anyone on the estate last night. I didn't want to frighten her by suggesting otherwise when there was no need.

I answered: *Ok, if you're sure. Text if you need anything.*

Cate confirmed she would, and we left the conversation there. I'd find out the next day why Cate sent everyone home (and I wouldn't be happy about it either). But it would lead to the most fantastical moment in both of our lives.

CHAPTER 4

August 18
5:55 p.m.

I spotted Cate and Riley meandering down the path to the loch the next morning. "Got a minute?" she called to me. She was talking to me, so she wasn't too mad, I surmised.

"I always have a minute for Lady Cate and Sir Riley," I answered.

"Mind taking a walk with us?" Cate inquired.

Uh-oh, I reflected, take a walk? What couldn't she tell me standing right here by the hedges? "Sure," I answered. "Everything okay, Cate?"

"Yes, everything is okay. I… Well…" Cate stammered around. Something made her nervous. Did she have another encounter with someone on the estate?

I stopped in my tracks, becoming concerned. "Cate, what is it?"

"Well," Cate repeated. She kicked the gravel around, avoiding eye contact with me.

"Yeah, I got that part," I joked in the hopes of prodding her to continue.

"The thing is..." She paused again. "I used the watch again... twice," she finally said.

"What? Twice? Cate, you promised," I chided, the disappointment clear in my voice.

"We won't get any information if we don't look for any!" Cate insisted.

"I can ask my grandfather when he gets back. He might have some information, he's worked here a long time."

"If he can't help, we have nothing."

"What if something happens to you while you're experimenting with this? Then we've really got nothing and no Cate either," I lectured. I shouldn't have but I couldn't help it. It just came out of my mouth, whether it should have or not. I didn't like messing around with something we had no idea about AND that had caused Cate to disappear somehow.

Cate frowned at me but continued. "But that's just it, I think I know what the watch is doing."

I heaved a sigh. Displeasure was likely apparent on my face, but I'd finish the discussion. "Okay, I'll bite, what do you think it's doing?"

"Two words: time travel!" Cate exclaimed. She grinned at me and raised her eyebrows.

"Time travel," I repeated. "Time travel? Cate, are you being serious?"

"Yes, I'm being serious. It sounds crazy, but just listen to what happened when I tried it yesterday."

She was serious. But it did sound crazy. She couldn't be serious, could she? But I was intrigued enough to find out what "proof" she had. "Okay, I'm not okay with you trying this out, but since you already did it, I'd like to hear why you presume you are time traveling."

"Okay!" Cate said. "Well, yesterday afternoon after lunch,

I decided that I would try the watch." Cate shot me a glance and held up her hands. "I was responsible and left a note, just in case!" She continued, "I went to the closet, the one I disappeared from, and I rubbed the watch. And it slowed down. I started by looking around the closet and bedroom. Nothing looked different to me. So, I ventured into the hallway. I made my way to where the hall branches off and I spotted two women walking down the hall, talking. They were dressed like chambermaids, but not like present-day maids. From what I glimpsed of them, I'd put their clothes around the 1850s, give or take."

Cate continued her story. Her voice accelerated as she spoke at lightning speed. "I didn't want them to see me, so I sneaked back to the bedroom and waited 'til they passed by. Then I heard someone else talking to them. I caught their names, and I wrote them down in my notes. I figured I could check the records to see if they worked here in the past. Anyway, I didn't stick around after that. Well, I did, only because I forgot the watch only works in certain areas and I tried to come back from the bedroom and that didn't work. Boy, did I panic. But then I remembered it worked in the closet, so I went back there and voila! It worked! I was back and only a few minutes had passed. Mrs. Fraser said she saw me ten minutes before I tried it."

"Then, I tried it last night, and…"

"Whoa, whoa, Cate, slow down," I interrupted.

My mind was reeling. I could barely comprehend what Cate babbled about. The idea made no sense. She had seen people from a previous era? Had she imagined it? The watch provided her a conduit for time travel?

"I need a moment to process what you just told me. You think you saw maids from the 1850s walking around the castle? Then you couldn't get 'back' but then you did? My head is spinning!"

"No!" Cate answered. "I don't THINK I saw them, I SAW them, Jack, plain as I see you standing in front of me."

I frowned at her. "You think I'm crazy," she said when I didn't answer.

"I don't know what to think, Cate," I admitted. I paused before adding, "But, no, I don't think you're crazy."

"I did see them" Cate repeated. "And they weren't mists or vapors or random shapes. They were plain as day people walking and talking.

"And you tried again last night?" I inquired. "Did you see the same people?"

"No!" Cate answered. "That's where things get interesting!" THAT'S where things get interesting, I wondered? Cate continued, "I remembered the watch always slowed down for me in the bedroom. So, I tried it there. No one was in the bedroom or sitting room, but my laptop and Riley were both gone. I took a walk around the castle to investigate and…"

"You took a walk around the castle to investigate?" I repeated as I cut her off. "Cate! You do not know where or when or whichever you are and you're gallivanting around like you're at the local fair!"

"I was careful, for the most part," Cate said with a shrug.

"What's that mean?" I inquired.

"I heard people in the sitting room. I peeked in. Several people were there. But they weren't dressed like they were from the 1850s, they were dressed like they were from the 1920s!"

"Now you're in the 1920s? With different people," I said, trying to make sense of things.

"Yes, they were different people. And yes, I'd put the year somewhere in the 20s based on the clothes they were wearing. Who says being a history professor never paid off, right?"

"Funny, yes," I answered, "seems right handy to identify the era you're time traveling to."

"Well, anyway, I didn't stick around, you know, to be safe and all. So, I was heading back up to the bedroom, but someone spotted me. A footman, I think. I raced to the bedroom and set the watch back to normal speed, and there I was, back in my bedroom in this time."

"You got caught?" I questioned; my eyes wide. My mind raced through all the possibilities where things didn't turn out as well as they did this time.

"No, I didn't get caught. I ran away and escaped!" Cate corrected.

"Oh, right, my mistake, someone spied you, somewhere in some time, but you ran away and escaped, sorry. I'm just envisioning the next time when maybe you can't run away."

Cate scowled. "Well, let's hope that doesn't happen. Anyway…"

I interrupted her again. "So, there will be a next time?

"Well…" Cate paused a moment. "Yes, I guess that is the long and short answer."

"Oh, Cate," I said with a shake of my head. "I realize I must sound like a broken record, but I don't think you should mess around with this stuff until we know what's going on, and maybe not even then. What if you get caught or stuck or whatever can happen with whatever is happening when you play with that watch? You're a nice lassie, Cate. I don't want anything to happen to you."

"I appreciate that. I do, but…"

"But you've no intention of listening?" I surmised.

"If I'm really time traveling, how exciting is that? It's an opportunity you can't pass up, right?"

"That's a big if, Cate. You're talking as though you're sure that's what's happening."

"Okay, point taken, we're not sure. But I strongly suspect

I'm right, nothing else makes sense! I mean, at first, I hypothesized seeing a spirit world or something, but two spirit worlds? That theory doesn't fit anymore."

My brain felt fuzzy. Nothing made sense. "Yeah, time travel makes way more sense than spirit worlds. Although, I missed the part where time travel makes any sense."

"Funny," Cate said with a groan.

We stared out at the loch as the conversation drew to a close. I could barely wrap my mind around what Cate had just told me. The proof she offered was frightening yet intriguing. But slipping back and forth through time? Could that be real?

I couldn't offer any further conjectures, and Cate and I disagreed about how to move forward. After a few moments, I said, "My grandfather is coming back at the end of the week. Can you at least not experiment any more with that until we can talk to him?" That gave us two days before we could find any answers. Though I wasn't sure how I felt about running this idea past Pap. Could I look him in the eye and say the words time travel?

Cate's answer isn't at all what I expected. "If you just saw how it worked, I think you'd…" she began.

Saw how it worked? The idea terrified me. Time traveling using a strange watch and little to no idea how it worked or what could go wrong? The phrase made me speak up before she finished her statement. "I'm not sure I want to see how it works. It's bizarre, even if your explanation is correct. It's downright scary if you ask me."

"But I think if you tried it, you'd see that it's…" she tried again.

"Cate," I chided.

"I just think…"

"Caaaaaate," I chided again.

She wrinkled her nose and crossed her arms. "This could

be the greatest discovery of all mankind and you don't want to even discover how it works!"

"We don't know WHAT it is, and can't you wait two short days?"

"It's possible your grandfather will not know anything!"

"Or if he'll have us fitted for straitjackets!"

"Just let me show you once how it works, and you can decide how dangerous it is for yourself."

"I feel like if I don't agree you're just going to do it on your own, anyway."

Cate didn't answer for a moment before she responded, "Probably."

I sighed. "As much as I don't want to do this, I'd rather not have you do it alone."

"So, you'll do it?" Cate asked with her eyebrows raised and an expectant grin on her face.

"Well, Lady Cate, since you're twisting my arm, I suppose I will."

Cate's grin broadened. "Meet me in the library after lunch."

After I agreed to the crazy plan, Cate and Riley returned to the castle. I spent the rest of the morning fretting over my decision. What had I gotten myself into? Time travel? No, it couldn't be. Time travel didn't exist! Whatever was going on with the watch, time travel wasn't it. But then what had Cate seen? Who were the people? My stomach twisted in knots.

As I sat down at the table for lunch, I wondered if I could stomach the meal. With each bite, I felt one step closer to doom. Perhaps I should call this off. Nay, then Lady Cate would go on her own and I couldn't let that happen. I wouldn't.

I wandered upstairs after lunch. My hand shook as I knocked on the library door.

"Come in!" Cate's voice called from the other side.

"Reporting for duty," I said with a salute as I entered the room.

"You will NOT be disappointed," Cate said as she leapt from her chair. "Come on!" She rushed out the door. "At least I hope not," she murmured.

"I hope I'm still around not to be," I said, only half-joking.

Cate made a face at me. "Sorry, bad joke. Just making sure you really want to do this!

"Out of the two of us, I don't expect it's ME who doesn't want to do it."

"Okay, I'll admit this is not the greatest idea I've ever had, but I'd rather you not mess around with this stuff alone."

We navigated the halls to the bedroom. "Come on!" Cate exclaimed. She pushed through the door and headed straight for the closet. "Close the door," she instructed. "Okay, here we go!"

Cate held the timepiece in front of her and rubbed it. She glanced up at me, a smile on her face. She opened her mouth to speak but...

Even now, I'm not sure I witnessed what I actually witnessed next. Before Cate could speak, she disappeared right before my eyes. One second she was standing in front of me, the next she was gone. My throat went dry, and my stomach somersaulted.

Within seconds, Cate reappeared in front of me.

"Cate!" I exclaimed.

"Jack! Sorry, I'm not sure what I was thinking. I lost you when the watch slowed down. I don't know why I assumed we'd just both go. Perhaps we both need to touch the watch. Let's try that."

How was she so calm? She yammered on as though she hadn't just disappeared! I, on the other hand, remained terrified! "Cate, you just disappeared in front of my eyes. One minute you were here, the next you were gone. Sorry, I need a minute. I mean, I realize you disappeared once before, but not right in front of my eyes! That was... freakish!"

Nothing deterred Cate. "Here," she responded, "try holding on to the watch with me, and maybe then I won't disappear!"

She wasn't going to take no for an answer. I reached out to take hold of the watch. I tried to steady my shaking hand as I wrapped my hand around Cate's.

"Okay, now rub it," Cate instructed.

I followed her instructions, both of us touching the timepiece's face. The second hand slowed, coming almost to a complete stop. "You made it!" Cate exclaimed as the second hand crept by.

I wondered about that. I pressed my hands all over my body to ensure I was really there. "I did, I guess," I admitted.

"Wanna look around?" Cate said with a grin.

"Do I have a choice?" I inquired.

"Nope, come on! We won't stay long but see if you notice anything different," Cate said.

Cate inched open the closet door and peeked into the bedroom. Spotting no one, Cate pushed the door open. I glanced around the room as we stepped into it. "I didn't recognize much as different in this room. Only that the lamps are missing, which makes sense if we are in the 1800s," Cate said.

I couldn't find my voice. I nodded in response.

"Let's check in the hall," Cate suggested. She pressed her ear to the bedroom door. After a moment, she nudged it open and glanced up and down the hall. She motioned for me to follow as she stepped into the hallway. "Let's head toward the front stairs," she whispered.

I nodded again. We crept toward the corner. Cate began to tell me she'd seen the maids in this area yesterday. I overheard a noise in the hall as Cate took another step toward the corner.

I grabbed Cate's arm and pulled her back around the corner. I pressed a finger to my lips to signal Cate to be quiet. Cate glanced around the wall, then signaled me to look, too.

Three women approached us. Two of them appeared to be maids, and the third carried a large set of keys around her waist. Was she the mistress of the house, I wondered? I couldn't believe my eyes. They did appear to be from another era. I confirmed silently to Cate that I spotted them and motioned for us to return to the bedroom.

Cate nodded, and we crept back to the room. I eased the door shut. Voices approached. We froze as the women passed our location, hidden by the closed door. The voices faded down the hall.

"Should we head back?" Cate inquired.

I'd never heard more beautiful words. "Yes, please, that's enough excitement for one day," I whispered.

Cate took a step toward the closet before she stopped. "This is where I was yesterday when I couldn't get the watch to work…" she began.

I interrupted her. "Let's talk about this after we're back."

"Oh, right, okay," Cate answered. We shut ourselves in the closet and clasped our hands over the watch. We rubbed the face with our thumbs. The second hand sped up and returned to normal speed. "Okay, that should be it. I told you! Those people are real. Do you believe me now?"

"I witnessed it with my own eyes, but I still can't say I accept it."

"Amazing, isn't it? Encountering people who shaped the history of this castle. It's every historian's dream to go back in history."

"I'm not sure I would call it a dream."

"There isn't a historian alive who wouldn't give anything

for five minutes in a room with some of the biggest influencers in history."

"There must be a reason no one knows about this, Cate. I don't think we should use this thing or tell anyone about it. Maybe my grandfather will have some information."

"Okay, okay, I promise not to use it. I feel better knowing someone else experienced this. Now I'm sure I'm not crazy."

"Oh, I experienced it, all right. You're not crazy. Or if you are, so am I."

"Mass hysteria?" Cate joked. "I don't think that's the case here."

"How are you so excited about this? That's enough excitement for the day. Time for me to put my own shape on the castle, starting with those bushes."

"Okay, yes, you're right. And I've got to document that experience."

"Okay, Cate. And you promise, no more 'trips,' right?"

"This time I promise!" Cate flashed a smile. "Scouts honor!" she said, holding up three fingers. "Oh, wait, while you're here, would you mind carrying this box of papers to my room? It's kind of heavy, I never got the chance to finish looking through it and I'd like to."

I picked up the box, glad to be back to normal work. My mind felt numb. Various thoughts flitted through it, but I could concentrate on none of them. What had we just experienced? Was Cate correct? Had we time traveled? How? How did the timepiece trigger this movement through time?

It all seemed too fantastic to be real. Surely this could not be the case. But what else explained it? I dropped the box next to Cate's chaise and pondered everything for another moment. With a shake of my head, I left the room and darted down a set of servant's stairs. I pushed through the door into the fresh afternoon air.

With a deep inhale, I attempted to stop my nerves from

overwhelming me and bringing my lunch up from my stomach. The entire experience still left my knees weak, even after some distance from it. I took another deep steadying breath before I staggered to the back garden.

My tools still lay scattered on the ground from my morning's trimming. With a hard swallow, I picked up my trimmers and continued working on the row of bushes I'd started earlier. With each snip, I felt a little better. Maybe the normalcy helped, or perhaps the shock was waning. Either way, I improved.

I struggled to push the experience from my mind. My brain returned to it every so often. I couldn't stop myself from dwelling on it. Yet, I had to or else I'd drive myself insane.

I managed to finish the afternoon without giving it too much further thought. As I ate dinner with the Frasers, I dreaded the meal's conclusion. I'd soon be left to my own devices and likely a sleepless night.

Two days, I pondered as I slogged through the door into my cottage. Two more days before I could speak to Pap in person about this. It was NOT something I wanted to do over the phone. Did I even want to consult him? As I lay in bed that night, I imagined the conversation. "Hi, Pap. Say, do you know anything about that old MacKenzie timepiece controlling time? Cate and I have been time traveling with it. We've been to the 1850s and Cate's also gone to the 1920s."

I imagined what a straitjacket might feel like when Pap inevitably locked me away for my own good. My stomach somersaulted at the mere thought of discussing this with my grandfather. Maybe I'd let Cate do the explaining. She was, after all, the historian.

CHAPTER 5

August 18
9:13 p.m.

*T*ime dragged by as I waited for Pap's return. My mindset toggled between acceptance of Cate's theory and utter disbelief. When Friday night rolled around, I drove to the airport to pick up Pap. As I leaned against the car awaiting his arrival, I considered springing the topic as we drove home. Perhaps it would be easier without making eye contact, I reflected.

That idea seemed terrible the moment I spotted Pap ambling toward me, dragging that little plaid suitcase behind him. He waved and grinned. I returned his wave as my mind soured at the idea of discussing this with him.

"Welcome home," I said as I clapped him on the back. I tossed his luggage in the boot and slid behind the wheel as he buckled his seatbelt in the passenger's seat. "How was the trip?"

"Refreshing," he admitted.

We sat in silence for a few miles. "How are things here? You seem quiet, Jackie."

I frowned. Pap knew me too well. "Busy," I hedged. "Hey, Cate had a few questions she hoped to ask you for a book she's writing. She also had a few questions about the castle and its history. Would you mind a visit with her?"

"Not at all," Pap answered. "Tomorrow good?"

"Sure," I answered, relieved to have it set.

We spent the remainder of the car ride discussing Pap's trip. I spent the rest of the night tossing and turning.

The next day brought a rainy Saturday to the area. Cool and damp weather kept everyone indoors. With no tasks able to be completed outside, Lady Cate offered the Frasers the day off. I texted her mid-morning and informed her my grandfather was home and requested a dinner meeting.

Cate answered almost immediately: *Sure... where?*

Pap suggested the castle, so I asked Cate if that was okay. After a moment, Cate responded: *Yes, that will work. No promises on dinner... I'm a terrible cook :P*

I figured. More than once I'd caught Lady Cate with a bowl of cereal for dinner when Mrs. Fraser wasn't cooking. I feared for my stomach, so I answered: *See you around 4? I can cook... you two can talk.*

Cate didn't hesitate with her response: *Deal... I'd politely decline and cook myself but no one wants to eat my cooking*

I sent an emoticon as a response; glad I had offered to cook. At least we wouldn't starve before Pap sent us to the funny farm. Given the new dinner plan, I had a bit of shopping to do. I hopped in the shower and headed to the market.

As I made my purchases, I wondered why I hadn't requested an earlier dinner. The suspense might kill me before time traveling did. Time traveling, my mind refused to believe that's what we were doing. Yet in two days I still hadn't come up with any other explanations.

Around three, I couldn't wait any longer. I loaded my groceries into the car as I dodged the raindrops and drove to Pap's and picked him up. We arrived a bit early at the castle. The rain poured down in a steady stream as I used the brass doorknocker, hoping it was loud enough for Cate to hear it. She opened the door almost immediately. She, too, must have been on pins and needles.

"Lady Cate!" I greeted her with a theatrical bow, careful not to spill any groceries from my bag.

"Come in and get dry!" Cate said. "Good to see you again, Mr. Reid, and thank you for coming!"

"It sure is wet out there. How are you enjoying our lovely weather, Sir Riley?" I asked as I scratched his chin.

"He doesn't mind the rain so much, he's all boy," Cate answered. "At least not when it's not thundering. He hates that."

I was ready to get the show on the road, so I didn't mince words. "Shall we head to the kitchen?"

"Sure, oh, and thank you again for offering to cook," Cate said.

"I was worried you'd cook cereal for dinner," I teased her.

"Oh, come on, I'm not THAT bad," Cate retorted. "I'd have opted for peanut butter and jelly at least!"

"Oh boy, I wish I hadn't offered. We really missed out, Pap!"

Pap chimed in, "I'd have taken anything this pretty lassie fed me. I'm not picky." Always a sucker for a pretty face, my Pap was.

"Thank you!" Cate said. "How was your trip?" Cate asked as we traversed through the castle halls to the kitchen.

"Great," Pap answered. "Nice to get away."

We arrived in the kitchen and Pap took his old seat at the

kitchen table. I set the groceries down and started to gather all my utensils. Cate offered to help, but I'd rather she do the talking to Pap than me, so I declined.

Cate sat down across from Pap. "Well, thanks for coming. I'm not sure if Jack mentioned it, but I'm putting together materials to write a book about the castle's history, and I figured you might be a good source of information. So, I'd like to ask you a few questions if you don't mind," Cate began.

Really, I thought? She's going to drag this out even further and ask about mundane things? I couldn't take another delay.

"Aw, come on, Cate," I said. "Skip to the juicy stuff. Ask him about your theory about that watch of yours."

Cate shot daggers at me from across the room. "I wasn't going to lead with that, but okay. I guess the real reason I wanted to talk to you, not that the other reason isn't legit, it is, but, well, I mentioned to you before that the watch was slowing down. You looked at it and told me nothing was wrong with it, which I now agree with because I deduced the watch should operate that way."

Wow, the way she stammered around, really gave away how nervous she was. I wished she'd get to the point so I could find out if we were crazy or not.

Pap continued to stare at her as she spoke, without offering much response. It made Cate even more nervous, and she continued to babble. "Well, what I mean to say is, Jack mentioned to you that I guessed friction induced it because I developed a habit, a tic, no pun intended." She gave a nervous laugh. "Of rubbing it and I postulated maybe that somehow messed with the internal workings. But now my theory is it's not just some random event, but that it's the watch's purpose…"

This couldn't go on. It would be tomorrow morning

before Cate got to the point. I interrupted her stammering. "Oh, for heaven's sake, Cate! She presumes we're time traveling by slowing the watch down, Pap. Ever heard of anything like that?"

There, I said it. Now I could be the one committed when Pap realized how insane we were.

Cate's face reddened. "Yes, that's what I concluded," she admitted. "That's my theory. Nothing made sense, but I kept seeing random people dressed in old-fashioned clothing when the watch was slow. Am I just going crazy?"

Pap chuckled. Here it comes, I figured. He's about to ask if she's had mental issues in the past.

"So, you figured it out, young lassie? Good for you! Lady MacKenzie didn't know if you'd be bright enough to catch on to it. She didn't leave you with many clues. Wondered if the secret might be best left to die with her since she couldn't tell you herself. Said if you were clever, you'd figure out the secret. She had faith that a MacKenzie could solve it."

I couldn't believe my ears. Did Pap say what I think he did? Did he just admit to Lady Cate that she was, in fact, correct and time travel existed?

"Wait a minute," I said as I approached the table. "She's RIGHT?"

"HEY!" Cate countered. "You saw it, too! And you agreed with my theory!"

"Well, it's a shock to hear it confirmed that we were actually time traveling."

"We?" Pap asked, raising an eyebrow at me. "Well, you're off to a right start, I'd say."

"Yes," Cate informed him, "we tried it together. Well, after a total fail when I disappeared for a few seconds without him."

"As I said, you're off to a good start. You figured out quite a lot, young Cate."

"I'm just shocked that I was right. I mean, I was convinced of my theory, but how has this been such a well-kept secret?"

"Ah, good question. The family never speaks of this secret to anyone outside of themselves. And whatever Reid is working on the estate."

Pap continued with his story. "Long ago, when the castle was built, the new owners detected what some called anomalies. This led to the rumors of the castle being haunted. And the builder, Douglas MacKenzie, you've no doubt read his name during your research, was the curious sort. He, along with his construction manager and later estate manager, Jaime Reid, my ancestor, spent countless hours studying these anomalies. Almost drove them crazy, but after some work, Douglas devised a mechanism that could interact with what he termed 'rips' in the 'fabric of time.' He, along with Jaime, built the watch and used their invention as a mechanism to control these rips.

"The secret has been passed from generation to generation. Always passed verbally, never written. You understand, if the wrong person discovered it, it could lead to disaster. The preceding caretaker always passed the secret to their heir. This time was different. No one knew what you'd be like and no one could find you before Lady MacKenzie passed. She tasked me with guarding the secret until we were sure you'd be able to take on the responsibility."

"So," Cate began. "Wow, I'm sorry, I need a minute. I have so many questions! I just… I can't believe it. I mean I've done it, I've time traveled, but I still can't believe it."

I stirred my stew and added, "You and me, both. It's still surprising even after experiencing the phenomenon for myself."

"Lady MacKenzie knew, did her mother, Mary, also know?"

"Aye, lassie. I worked on the estate when Lord MacKenzie

passed and left the responsibility to Lady Mary since Lady Gertrude was too young."

"You mentioned not knowing if I'd be suitable to take on the responsibility? The secret could have died with Gertrude?" Cate inquired.

"Aye, as I mentioned, it's quite a responsibility and Gertrude would have rather seen the secret die with her than fall into the wrong hands. Not that she doubted you, but never having met you and not knowing anything about you, well, I guess she erred on the side of caution. You can imagine the repercussions if this fell into the hands of someone who would exploit it for their own gain."

Cate remained silent a moment before responding. "Yes, I can see your point. I found some journals Mary kept from when she had inherited the watch and, while they were redacted, she describes the secret in the same way: as a responsibility. I see it as a gift, what historian wouldn't love to immerse themselves in an era not theirs. The learning potential is unlimited."

"You're eager, I see, but you must temper your eagerness with caution. You must be careful with this 'gift,' Cate, you don't always understand the repercussions of changing too much in the past. You must follow the rules that have been passed through the generations. Striking a balance and following those rules are the responsibility that both Mary and Gertrude spoke of."

"I see your point, again. I guess my enthusiasm got ahead of me."

"Aye, it can be exciting, but you have to be careful. Got to consider what you're doing before you start changing things. Caution like that requires a cool head and a steady hand," Pap warned her.

Thank goodness, I thought, perhaps Pap could talk some sense into the eager lassie.

"Do you know how many 'rips' exist?" Cate asked.

"I'm not sure if we ever had an exact count. The rips exist in different places throughout the castle. Different rips connect to different times. Lady Gertrude disliked traveling, unlike her mother. If I remember, Lady Mary identified at least four spots."

"Do you remember where these spots exist?"

"Aye, one of them in the bedroom Lady Gertrude stayed in, one of them in the bedroom down the hall, another in the downstairs office, that's a tricky one, never know who might be in there, and the fourth she found exists in another bedroom, the one they call the Blue Room."

Cate remained silent another moment and Pap added, "May be more, those were the ones she identified. Her husband took ill and passed her the watch and the secret with little information. Oh, that reminds me there's a hallway that seems to work in any time to return, handy to remember in case of an emergency. It's the one that looks out on the back garden."

Handy in an emergency, I pondered. I didn't want to find out what types of emergencies required a universal time travel portal.

"The secret is passed down in BOTH the MacKenzie and Reid families?" Cate asked.

"Yes. The Reids' duty is always to protect this secret right along with the MacKenzies."

Uh-oh. My mind spun out of control at the last statement. Reids' duty? This didn't sound good.

"So, you helped Mary and Gertrude protect the secret?"

"Aye, lassie. Took many a trip with Lady Mary back in my younger days. As I said, Lady Gertrude was not a fan of traveling as much as her mother." He turned to me as I sprinkled salt into my stew. "Now, I'm officially passing the mantle to you, lad. The secret is now yours and Cate's and it's up to you to protect it and Cate."

Oh, no. I knew it didn't sound good.

"Thanks, Pap, I have my work cut out with this one," I said, nodding my head toward Cate.

Cate laughed. "Hey, I'm not THAT bad. He's been doing a good job so far," she informed Pap. "So, only the three of us know?"

"That's right, lassie."

"Mr. and Mrs. Fraser?"

"Charlie and Emily? Nay. I dare say she might faint dead away if she found out."

Cate laughed, though I agreed with Pap's statement. I was glad I didn't tell Emily Fraser anything about Cate's disappearance a few days ago.

"That reminds me," Cate said, "once I 'traveled' back and when I came back, Mrs. Fraser said she'd just seen me. But I was gone for at least fifteen to twenty minutes. Does that make sense?"

"Aye, and a good observation on your part. When you travel, the time where you're from almost stands still. That's why the watch is slow. The watch keeps time from YOUR time. Now, I said ALMOST. We calculated the ratio to be about fifteen minutes in the past to one minute here. Tempting as it may be to spend a lot of time in the past, you must remember that you can't go disappearing from your own time for too long. People will wonder."

"Always keep an eye on YOUR time. It's the inscription on the watch and it was in Lady Gertrude's note. NOW it makes sense!" Cate exclaimed.

"Aye, lassie, that's right. The warning from Douglas MacKenzie himself. Had the phrase engraved on that watch to remind everyone."

After a breath, Cate continued. "On a different note, do

you know why my family branch became estranged? I found a family bible with an inkblot over my branch of the family. As you mentioned, I wasn't easy to find. I found evidence that Gertrude visited my parents before my birth, but then it seems like all contact was cut off and our side was blotted out in the family bible."

"I cannae help you there, lassie. Lady Gertrude never mentioned it, never discussed your side. She knew your family, but not where to find you. I got the impression that your grandparents moved and changed their names around when a spot of trouble cropped up. The castle's secret was almost discovered. Perhaps moved to protect your family from being sought by any undesirable people. My guess is Lady Gertrude stayed away after your birth, just to keep your family safe."

"That makes sense and seems reasonable. This is a lot to digest, but thank you for the information."

"Well, there you have it, Lady Cate. Your theory was right, mystery solved! Now you can relax!" I said as I delivered piping hot bowls of my famous stew to the table.

"Relax? My mind is whirling with the possibilities! Do you like history, Jack?" Cate asked.

"Oh, boy," I answered with a groan. "You sure you don't want your old job back, Pap?"

"Oh, come on, Jack, the adventures are just beginning," she said with a gleam of mischief in her eye.

And boy, did she mean it. Well, that's the story of how Cate and I discovered time travel. I hoped since then that it would fade away as a little-discussed, seldom used anomaly of the castle. That wouldn't be the case. So, in this journal, I'll log everything in case we need a record. Of course, as Pap mentioned, no one should ever read it, but at least I can keep my thoughts straight. Until next time…

Stay up to date with all my news! Be the first to find out about new releases first, sales and get free offers! Sign up for the newsletter now!

Now that you know the secret of Dunhaven Castle, join Jack for his second story! Help Jack and Cate solve a murder in Murder in the Tower! There's even a little mystery for Riley, too!

Want to read Cate's full story? Try The Secret of Dunhaven Castle to learn about Cate's journey from Aberdeen, USA to Scotland!

Like supernatural suspense? Try the Shadow Slayers series, a fast-paced page-turner! Book one, Shadows of the Past, is available now!

Ready for adventure? Travel the globe with Maggie Edwards in search of her kidnapped uncle and Cleopatra's Tomb.

Book one, Cleopatra's Tomb, in the Maggie Edwards Adventure series is available now!

Love immersing yourself in the past? Lenora Fletcher can communicate with the dead! Can she use her unique skill to solve a mystery? Find out in Death of a Duchess, Book 1 in the Duchess of Blackmoore Mysteries.

A NOTE FROM THE AUTHOR

Dear Reader,

Thank you for reading this book! If you're already a Cate Kensie fan, I hope you enjoyed reading Jack's perspective! The Secret Keepers: Jack's Journal #2 is already available. If you enjoyed this book, check out Murder in the Tower today!

If you're new to the Cate Kensie Mysteries, welcome! I hope you enjoyed the first installment of Jack's Journal. Continue with Jack's Journal #2 or check out The Secret of Dunhaven Castle, Cate's version of the story!

Keep reading for a sneak peek of Murder in the Tower: Jack's Journal #2.

All the best, Nellie

MURDER IN THE TOWER: JACK'S JOURNAL #2 SYNOPSIS

A centuries-old murder. An innocent man convicted.
If you could change the past, would you?

When Lady Catherine Kensie stumbles upon a sordid tale of murder on the estate's grounds and learns her ancestor was convicted despite having an alibi, she's determined to get to the bottom of things.

While cautious estate manager, Jack Reid, isn't sure there's anything to be solved, he agrees to investigate.

Together, the time-traveling duo slip back in time and become embroiled in the murder investigation and a dangerous game of cat and mouse.

Can they save an innocent man's life? Or will Dunhaven Castle claim another victim?

Read *Murder in the Tower* now by clicking here!

MURDER IN THE TOWER: JACK'S JOURNAL #2 EXCERPT

I waited for a few moments for Randolph to disappear before I began my search of the downstairs. I popped in and out of several rooms, this time checking each with a discerning eye. I continued down the hall toward the library. My eyes scanned the room as I entered. Just inside the door, a scrap of paper lay on the floor. I snatched it from the hardwood and glanced at it for a moment before continuing my search.

I did a double-take as I recognized the addressee. My eyes widened as I read the words scrawled on the grainy paper in black ink.

> *Catherine–I must see you, it's urgent. Meet me at the loch at 3:30.*
> *-Randolph*

Oh, no. My stomach dropped and my mouth went dry. Randolph wasn't meeting Cate. This was a ruse. One Cate was most likely unaware of. Whatever purpose was behind it could not be honorable. I cursed allowing her out of my sight as I rushed from the library to the nearest door. I sprinted down the path to the loch.

As I approached, I overheard the sound of an argument. "Let go!" Cate screamed.

My heart pounded in my chest as I raced toward the water. I crested the hill with the loch lying below me. Andrew held Cate by the arms. She struggled against him, but he backed her into the loch. With one final shove, Cate toppled backward, tumbling into the icy waters.

She flailed as she struggled to stay afloat, but the heavy fabric she wore proved too much for her. I raced headlong toward the water's edge as Cate slipped below the surface.

Want to read more? Click here to help Jack and Cate solve the murder in *Murder in the Tower*!

Made in the USA
Las Vegas, NV
29 March 2024